D0411212

Nipper
McFee
In Trouble with Great Aunt Twitter

For Morgan
R.I.

For Albert
M.W.

Reading Consultant: Prue Goodwin, Lecturer in literacy and children's books

ORCHARD BOOKS
338 Euston Road, London NW1 3BH
Orchard Books Australia
Hachette Children's Books
Level 17/207 Kent Street, Sydney NSW 2000

First published in 2010 by Orchard Books
First paperback publication in 2011

A CIP catalogue record for this book is available from the British Library.

ISBN 978 1 40830 216 3 (hardback)
ISBN 978 1 40830 224 8 (paperback)

1 3 5 7 9 10 8 6 4 2 (hardback)
1 3 5 7 9 10 8 6 4 2 (paperback)
Printed in China

Orchard Books is a division of Hachette Children's Books, an Hachette UK company.

www.hachette.co.uk

Nipper McFee

In Trouble with Great Aunt Twitter

Written by ROSE IMPEY
Illustrated by MELANIE WILLIAMSON

Nipper McFee wasn't a bad cat.
He didn't go looking for trouble
– trouble came looking for him.

Today, trouble was wearing a fur coat and carrying a lot of shopping.

Ooops!

Nipper didn't see trouble coming, because he was far too busy having a good time.

Oh, my claws and paws!

Great Aunt Swanker lived in the flat next door. She was a good friend of Nipper's mother. "Mark my words," she told Mrs McFee, "that kitten will come to a very bad end."

Poor Mrs McFee was in despair.
"Why, oh why, can't you be more like your brother Monty?" she asked.

Nipper rolled his eyes.
He was not a fan of his brother Monty.

Monty and Nipper shared
a bedroom.
Every day Monty got up at
six o'clock to practise his
scales and polish his shoes.

He liked to do extra maths homework before his breakfast. Monty McFee was too good to be true.

Unfortunately, Nipper wasn't.
Nipper did not like singing,
he never polished his shoes
and he hated maths homework!
He liked playing in the street with
his friends: Will and Lil McClaw.

Most of all, he liked fighting with his enemies – the basement rats.

But not for much longer,
because Mrs McFee had a plan.
From now on, trouble would have
trouble finding Nipper.
He would be far too busy – singing!

Singing?!

"You can join your brother Monty in the church choir," she told Nipper. "That should keep you out of trouble."

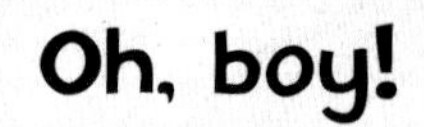

Will and Lil thought it was
the end of the world.
But Nipper didn't seem worried
because he had a plan of his own.

"Wait till old Miaowser hears me singing," he laughed. "He'll need a ton of cotton wool in his ears."

Sure enough, the moment Nipper
opened his mouth to sing,
Mr Miaowser asked, "Who
is that cat-erwauling?"
Nipper put up his paw and smiled.

But the choirmaster had a surprise for Nipper.
He would teach him to sing, even if it took every night of the week.

It was a cat-astrophe for Nipper! Staying behind every night was bad enough, but seeing those basement rats laughing at him was much worse.

When it was all over, Nipper was free to go home. But the rats were waiting for him outside, with cat-apults and peashooters!
"Get Nipper! " they shouted.

Those rotten rodents chased
Nipper down back alleys,
through car parks and under
flyovers – halfway across town.

News
Post
CAKES
CINEMA
HOTEL

Finally, they chased Nipper into the Cat-lick Car Wash and cornerered him.

But Nipper wasn't giving in
without a fight.

It was all out war and it looked as
if the rats might win.

Nipper couldn't hold on any longer, so he ducked behind a pick-up truck.
Just then, PC Poodle came round the corner.

The policeman got soaked to
the skin.
Nipper smiled as he watched the
rats get the trouble they deserved.
He hoped that would teach them:
Don't mess with Nipper McFee!

When Nipper got home he looked like something the cat had dragged in.

"Oh, my poor little kitten!" Mrs McFee cried, opening her paws.

Nipper was put straight to bed
with warm milk and honey and
a nice hot-water bottle.
And his brother Monty had to
wait on him.

The next day Nipper felt so poorly he could not go to school. He had completely lost his voice.

"From now on there'll be no more

late nights for my little kitten,"
Mrs McFee told him, lovingly.
"And no more choir practice!"
Nipper was *so* disappointed.

In Trouble with Great Aunt Twitter	978 1 40830 216 3
In Trouble with Growler Grimes	978 1 40830 217 0
In Trouble with Bertie Barker	978 1 40830 218 7
In Trouble with Mrs Lulu Lamb	978 1 40830 219 4
In Trouble with Mrs McFee	978 1 40830 220 0
In Trouble with Primrose Paws	978 1 40830 221 7
In Trouble with Susie Soapsuds	978 1 40830 222 4
In Trouble with PC Poodle	978 1 40830 223 1

All priced at £8.99